PANCAKES AND PICKLES

Written by
Sy Schimberg
Barron Schimberg

Illustrated by
Ringling College of Art and Design
Illustration Students

www.pancakespickles.com

All profits from the sale of this book will be donated to Miracle League of Manasota. Miracle League is an organization that provides people with disabilities the chance to play the game of baseball.

Create Space Publishers

Thank You Ringling College of Art and Design

We thank the 13 Ringling students who contributed their time and hard work towards illustrating <u>Pancakes and Pickles</u>. A special thank you to Livy Long, who helped organize the illustration process. We are amazed by your talents.

ILLUSTRATORS	ILLUSTRATIONS
Audrey Benjaminsen	H & P
James Cassettari	G & V
Angeline Chen	E & S
Anna Craig	M & R
Grace Elizabeth	J & U
Amanda Erb	L & Y
Audrey Gonzalez	C & F
Hannah Holmes	A & Q
Kyle Katterjohn	N & Z
Livy Long	D & T
Charlotte Mao	I & O
Victor Maury	K & X
Patu Phan	B & W

Pancakes and Pickles / written by Sy and Barron Schimberg
Illustrations by Ringling College of Art and Design Illustration Students

First published in the United States: 2013
Create Space Publishers

Dedication and Gratitude

I dedicate this book, <u>Pancakes and Pickles</u>, to Miracle League of Manasota. The Miracle League participants and volunteers are truly great people and I thank them for sharing so many valuable lessons with me, some of which are impossible to learn anywhere else.

I thank my brother, Hugh, for staying calm and not complaining when my father and I would sometimes take days handling the book.

Thank you mom for sticking by my side through the whole process and always encouraging me.

Behind the scenes, Sonika Fourie did an incredible job helping us format the book. Thank you.

Last, but not least, an extra thank you to my dad. If it weren't for my father, who helped me create the idea of <u>Pancakes and Pickles</u> when I was 5, and helped complete it when I was 12, you would never be reading the book now. It took a while and it sure wasn't easy, but we finally did finish the book, <u>Pancakes and Pickles</u>.

I hope you enjoy reading this book as much as we enjoyed writing it!

Sy Schimberg

www.miracleleaguemanasota.org

A Annabelle asked her aunt for some animal crackers.

Her aunt answered, "Absolutely, but you can't have animal crackers without anchovies!"

"Anchovies?" Annabelle argued. "Arrggggg!!!"

B

Billy bothered Bud for some bananas at the baseball game.

But Bud bellowed, "Bananas? You can't bite into bananas without broccoli!"

Billy barfed.

Christopher cried, "Can't I have cotton candy?"

The circus clown cackled, "Cotton candy is crazily compatible with clams casino."

Christopher couldn't comprehend.

Drew drafted a document designating dark chocolate is delicious.

Drew's dad declared, "Dark chocolate is delicious but only with deviled eggs!"

"You're deranged!" denounced Drew.

llie exclaimed to Ed, "Egg salad is extremely exciting!"

Ed emphasized, "Egg salad is only exciting with escargot!"

Ellie emphatically elected to exclude Ed.

Frank, the fireman, found Fynn fiddling with fudge.

Fascinated, Frank followed the fudge with fancy foie gras.

"Fudge with foie gras? Flabbergasting!" frowned Fynn.

Greg growled to the grumpy guy, "Guacamole is great."

The grumpy guy got up and gloated, "Great guacamole goes only with grits!"

Greg's guts grumbled.

Huey howled, "The honeydew Hal handed me was happily hip!"

Hal had a hilarious idea.

He hoped his honeydew hinted of horseradish.

Huey was horrified!

Isabella insisted on issuing ice cream in the island of Igeewa, inhabited by iguanas and icky monsters.

In addition, icky monsters always include Italian dressing in their ice cream!

"Interesting…" Isabella imagined.

Jane jumped for joy when Jackson jammed on jellybeans at Jazz Fest.

But when Jackson jumbled the jellybeans with jambalaya, Jane danced the jive!

The **k**night, **k**icking like a **k**angaroo, **k**nocked down the **k**umquat tree for the **K**ing's **k**umquat pie.

When the **K**ing became **k**nowledgeable of the **k**umquat pie, he **k**new **k**idney beans would be the **k**ey to its success.

The **k**night cackled, "Are you **k**idding me?"

Lucy loved her lollipops.

She licked and licked them all day long!

Then her friend Lynn said, "Here, try some liver with those lollipops. It's de-licious!"

Lynn laughed loudly.

M

Mr. Mack mushed marshmallows in his messy mouth.

His mommy made meatballs.

Mr. Mack's mommy mixed marshmallows and meatballs to make marshballs!

"Yuuum-my!" mumbled Mr. Mack.

Nick noticed nice nougat while noodling in the candy store.

Nick's Nana from Nantucket needed to introduce Nick to New England clam chowder.

Nick noted, "Nougat and New England clam chowder? Oh no!"

Ollie opened a jar of orange marmalade before his opera performance.

Olaf ogled at his old friend Ollie, "OMG! Try these outstanding oysters with your orange marmalade!"

Ollie said "Oy!"

 P

Patty proclaimed positively that pancakes are perfect!

Patty's Pop Pop pronounced that pancakes are possibly plain without pickles.

Patty panicked, "Pancakes and pickles? Preposterous!"

Queen **Q**uintessa **q**uietly cooked **q**uiche for her Majesty's **q**uartet.

Quickly, King **Q**uigly **q**uestioned his **q**ueen, "Where are the **q**uahog clams?"

"**Q**uiche and **q**uahog clams? **Q**uite a **q**uagmire."

Randy randomly remembered his mother's ravioli recipe for the family reunion.

Uncle Ralph recommended retrieving rhubarb for the recipe.

"Radical!" reported Randy.

Snyder snatched sardines from Stevie for a sandwich.

"Scrumptious!" Snyder stated.

Stevie secretly slipped Swiss cheese over the sardines.

Snyder screamed, "Something is seriously scary about this sandwich!"

Stevie slyly smiled.

Timmy tiredly took a taste of the tapioca pudding.

As it touched his tongue, Tom tried to trick Timmy into topping it with a tiny trout.

"Tapioca pudding and trout?" Timmy's temper tripled! "Totally tacky!"

"**U**ummm… **u**nder the **u**nicorn, **u**pon the **u**mbrella, is an **u**nusually **u**pside down cake," **u**ttered **U**rsula.

The **u**pside down cake was **u**nbelievable, **u**ntil…

Ulrich **u**nwrapped and added a **u**nique **u**rchin.

"**U**ghh!" **U**rsula was **u**pset.

iolet viewed Victor re-vamping his vonderful menu.

Violet intervened, "Vhere is the vanilla custard?"

Victor vondered, "Vhat vould happen if vee mixed vanilla custard vith venison?"

Violet vomited!

"I win!" wailed Willy. "I won wonderful waffles!"

"What?!" wondered Wendy. "What in the world would waffles be without wasabi?"

"Whoa," whispered Willy, "She's wacky!"

Xavier e**x**citedly e**x**claimed, "Pancakes and pickles are e**x**cellent."

E**x**cept...in **X**ena's establishment, e**x**tra pancakes and e**x**tra pickles were an e**x**tra e**x**pense.

Xavier e**x**pressed his e**x**citement by e**x**pelling **X**ena!

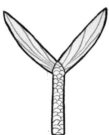

"Hey you... over yonder...yeah you...with the yellow yippy Yorkie. Have you ever yearned for yogurt?"

"Yes?"

"You know, yogurt is yummy with yellow fin tuna!"

"Yuck!"

Zany Zach zeroed in on a bizarre zucchini dish in Zimbabwe.

Zoe zestfully zoomed to Zach and exclaimed, "Zucchini is worth zillions with zero calorie caramel!"

"Zip it!!" buzzed Zach.

Made in the USA
Middletown, DE
27 November 2017